WONKENSTEIN
THE CREATURE
FROM MY
CLOSET

WONKENSTEIN

THE CREATURE
FROM MY
CLOSET

OBERT SKYE

Christy Ottaviano Books

Henry Holt and Company ✦ New York

Henry Holt and Company, LLC
Publishers since 1866
175 Fifth Avenue
New York, New York 10010
mackids.com

Henry Holt® is a registered trademark of
Henry Holt and Company, LLC.
Copyright © 2011 by Obert Skye
All rights reserved.

Library of Congress Cataloging-in-Publication Data
Skye, Obert.
Wonkenstein / Obert Skye. — 1st ed.
p.   cm. — (The creature from my closet ; 1)
"Christy Ottaviano Books."
Summary: Twelve-year-old Rob has stuffed his closet with old laboratory
experiments, unread books, and more, and when a creature emerges from
that chaos causing a great deal of trouble, Rob has to do such horrible things
as visit a library and speak at a school assembly to set things right again.
ISBN 978-0-8050-9268-4
[1. Monsters—Fiction. 2. Conduct of life—Fiction. 3. Books and
reading—Fiction. 4. Schools—Fiction. 5. Family life—Fiction.
6. Humorous stories.] I. Title.
PZ7.S62877Won 2011   [Fic]—dc22   2011004870

First edition—2011 / Designed by Véronique Lefèvre Sweet
Printed in August 2011 in the United States of America by
R. R. Donnelley & Sons Company, Harrisonburg, Virginia

1 3 5 7 9 10 8 6 4 2

For my dad,

quite possibly the greatest father ever

CONTENTS

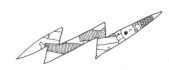

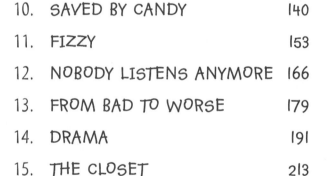

WONKENSTEIN

THE CREATURE

FROM MY

CLSET

CHAPTER 1

THE CLOSET DOOR

This is not your normal book. Normal books begin with things like "Once upon a time" or "Jimmy Pennyworth was a fine young man with a bright future, blah, blah, blah. . . ." And since you've read this far, you can clearly see that this book begins with neither of those.

My name is Robert Columbo Burnside. I got my first name from my mom's dad, my middle name from some TV detective my parents like, and my last name from my father. Our family is related to the man who invented sideburns—which really isn't that great a discovery.

Old people call me Bobby, my friends call me Rob, and my mother calls me Ribert—a name that is very embarrassing. Like the time when she yelled out for me at the store, she sounded like a frog. I had to hide just so Melanie Wolf wouldn't see it was me.

Of course, it was even more embarrassing when I tripped climbing out of the ball bin and smashed into Melanie as she was putting on lip gloss. The tube went halfway up her nose.

I'll have to cross Melanie off my list of girls who secretly might like me.

My dad doesn't call me Ribert. He calls me Robert, and he's a pretty good dad. His name is Earl, and he sells playground equipment. He's always smiling and talking about how he has the best job on earth.

Even though he's nice, he's also embarrassing. He always wears a suit and tie. Plus, he thinks everyone he meets is his new best friend.

I probably wouldn't write any of this down if it weren't for my oddly disturbing closet. But because of that, I've decided I should document some of the stuff going on in my life, for the sake of science and scientific study. Who knows? It could be important someday.

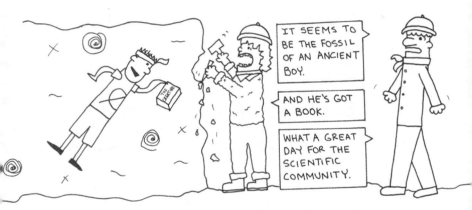

When I got my own room five years ago, there wasn't a door for the closet. So my dad went out and found a door at a garage sale that he thought worked perfectly. I thought it worked, but not perfectly. It's very heavy. I break into a sweat just trying to open it.

My dad claims the door's made of wood, but I'm pretty sure it's made out of lead. It also has a goofy sticker of a dumb pony with the word *SMILE* on it. We tried to scrape it off, but whoever owned the door before us painted over it with shellac, so now it's permanent.

I don't really care that much about the door, but there's one thing that really makes me uneasy, and that's the doorknob—it's big and gold, with the ornate engraving of a small, smiling, bearded man on it.

I've asked my dad to change the doorknob a thousand times, but he just says . . .

WHY SETTLE FOR REGULAR WHEN YOU CAN HAVE A DOORKNOB WITH CHARACTER?

I don't agree—the doorknob creeps me out. It seems like the little bearded man is always looking at me. Sometimes I have to put a towel over the doorknob just so I can change into my clothes.

I only mention the door because it probably has something to do with the condition of my closet. See, my closet's not really just a closet.

When I first got my own room, I wanted to turn my closet into a laboratory. But my parents wouldn't buy me a chemistry set, so I had to collect my own lab supplies. I took all the ketchup and relish and mustard from our refrigerator. I gathered all the cleaning supplies and shampoo I could find. And I took some of my mom's and sister's makeup when they weren't looking. Then I mixed the condiments and makeup with Play-Doh and mud in my closet and tried to discover a cure for everything from chapped lips to hangnails. I never really cured anything except cleanliness.

After I failed at that, my closet became just a place where I could shove things I didn't want to bother with anymore—things like my sister.

Libby is my slightly older sister. As far as sisters go, she's pretty close to the most painful one ever created. She's always looking in the mirror and commenting on how *beautiful* she is. When she was in sixth grade, she lost the spelling bee because of her vanity. The word was *beautiful*, and she spelled it . . .

Libby isn't allowed anywhere near my closet
unless I'm pushing her in. Besides, she claims it
makes weird noises when I'm not around. That
doesn't surprise me. I put everything in my closet—
toys I've outgrown, clothes that no longer fit, sports
equipment I was never good with, trash, and all the
hundreds of books my mother tries to make me
read. Books like . . .

I'm not sure how you feel about books, but me,
I'm torn. My mother used to work at a bookstore
and collected tons of books. Now our basement is
crammed with them. Which means that every week
or so, my mother wanders down into the basement
and picks out books for me and my sister to read.
Libby always acts all fake and happy about it. Then
she just throws them back down into the basement.

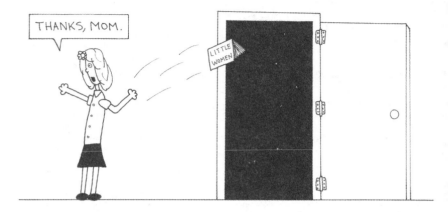

I also have a younger brother. His name is Kevin, but when he was born, I couldn't say Kevin so I called him Tuffin. It stuck, and now that's what everyone calls him. He's not the worst little brother, but he's cuter than I am, and my parents seem to settle arguments these days based on who's cuter. So I always try extra hard to be out of the house whenever he breaks things.

I can't stand when my mother gives Tuffin books.
Tuffin always looks at his book and then spends the
rest of the week begging me to read it to him. But
he's hard to read to because he makes up words
and insists they're in the book. And if I don't read   .
the words just the way he wants me to, he throws
a fit.

I throw all the books my mother gives me into
my closet. But I'll be honest, even I'm a little
embarrassed by how messy it is. In fact, last night
when I looked over at my closet, I was shocked.
Things were spilling out, and I could smell something

disgusting. I was going to get up and close my closet door, but it seemed like a lot of work. So I just shut my eyes and pushed my face into my pillow to block the smell.

I still couldn't fall asleep, so I tried counting fried chickens. My dad always says that it's way better to count fried chickens instead of sheep because then when you wake up you'll be hungry and ready to take on the day. I guess it works because chicken number twenty-three was the last chicken I remembered.

CHAPTER 2

SATURDAY CHORES

Saturday started out normal enough. I woke up around ten, helped myself to a bowl of cold cereal, told my mom I had done my Saturday chores, and went outside to hang out with some of the kids in the neighborhood. My street is pretty good as far as friends are concerned. There are kids my age in almost every house, and I'm friends with most of them.

My favorite friend is Trevor. We've been best friends for about twelve years. His glasses are

nearly always crooked, and he talks a lot, but he also goes along with most of my ideas, and I don't mind going along with his. Another good thing about Trevor is that he's worse than me at most sports, which makes me look better than I am.

My friends and I usually hang out in front of my house on a big, rocky island in the middle of the cul-de-sac. The island has three palm trees and a bunch of big, scratchy bushes, and it's covered with rocks and two patches of grass.

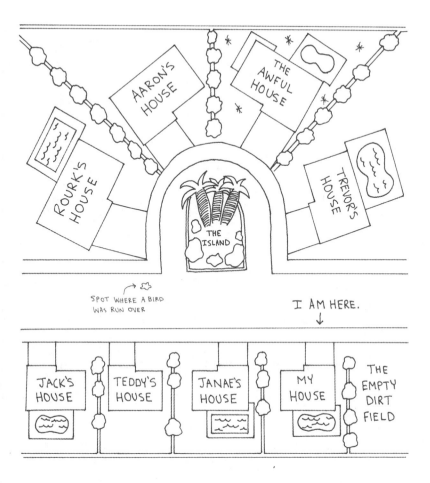

Most Saturdays we all gather at the island or the empty dirt field by my house. Sometimes we dig holes or play football or talk about the girls in our neighborhood. And sometimes we dare each other to go knock on the door of the Awful House.

The Awful House is the one house on our street
that doesn't really match. It was built a long time
ago, before there was a neighborhood, and now it
just sits there with a grown-over yard and a rickety
windmill, looking old and odd. Mr. Pang lives there
with his big son, Oscar. We all call Oscar Ogre.
Once Aaron actually opened the front screen door
of the Awful House and stuck his head inside. Aaron
said he could hear babies crying, but Aaron says a
lot of things that aren't exactly true.

So, it was early Saturday, and we weren't quite bored enough to be bothering with the Awful House yet. We were talking about why Janae Welt was too cute to like any of us when my father came home. He had a huge metal thing in the back of his truck, and he was smiling wider than usual.

Since my dad is in the playground business, he sometimes brings home playthings for us to test out. Once he brought a huge ball with handles on it called the Whirl-Sphere. My dad said it was going to be the next big thing. He had me and my friends get on it and then pushed us down a hill.

We got so beaten up they had to discontinue the Whirl-Sphere. Another time my dad brought home a slide with rollers on it. He said it was going to make all other slides look stupid. Well, I got my clothes and skin pinched in it. Aaron got his sweater pulled up over his head, Trevor's shoelaces got stuck, and Jack lost some of his hair. Rourk made things even worse by plowing down through everyone. In the end, it was us, not other slides, who looked stupid.

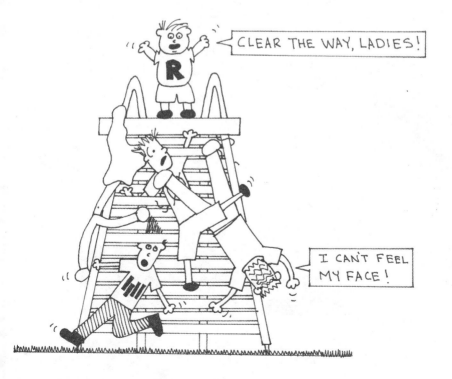

Today my dad brought home a Jump-A-Roo. He told us that if we jumped on it and pretended like we were having fun, he would take our picture and we could be on the front of a playground catalog. My friends liked that. They all started jumping and grinning big, fake, cheesy grins while my dad took pictures. Even Jack, who prides himself on never smiling, smiled.

I was just about to get my
turn when Tuffin fell through
the bars and Jack accidentally
jumped on his ankle. Jack
said it wasn't him, but thanks
to my dad taking pictures,
we had proof.

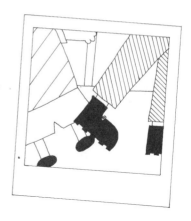

I had to take Tuffin inside to calm him down and
get my mom to help him. My mom, by the way, is
completely the opposite of my dad—my dad likes to
go, go, go, and my mom likes to nap. I love her, but
it's a rare moment in our house when my mom isn't
lying on the couch sleeping. She went to the doctor
once to see why she was always tired. They ran a
bunch of tests, and in the end, the doctor said she
was exhausted because she was a mother and had
three kids to look after.

My mother was so upset Tuffin got hurt that
she got up from the couch and began rummaging

through the hall closet for some bandages. While rummaging, she happened to look into my room and notice that I hadn't actually done my Saturday chores. She threw a bigger fit than Tuffin was throwing. She also made me clean my room while my friends all posed for pictures and jumped on the one piece of equipment my dad had brought home that was actually fun.

It took me two hours, including break times, to shove all of my things into my closet. I crammed everything in with all the old stuff from my laboratory. When I was done, I could barely close the closet door, and Beardy looked fat.

I took some Silly Putty I had found while cleaning and shoved it into his face.

When I told my mom I was finished, she just snored, so I went back outside. My dad had

stopped taking pictures a while ago, and Jack had
accidentally punctured the tube with a lawn dart. So
all I could do was hold on to the bars and sort of
hop. It wasn't that fun.

When I went to sleep that night, I noticed that
the Silly Putty had fallen off my closet doorknob
and Beardy was smiling at me again. I thought
about getting out of bed and picking the putty up,
but Fred, our parrot, flew into my room and I didn't
want to scare him away. When we brought Fred

home years ago, he busted out of his cage, and we haven't been able to catch him since. So Fred flies around the house as he pleases, and he sits up in the beams of our ceiling and poops on things. He only comes down for food at night when everyone's asleep.

We also have a dog named Puck. He's possibly the world's fattest dog and really doesn't do anything besides lick up bird poop and whine to go outside—which is a problem because he doesn't fit through the door easily.

Neither one of our pets is going to win an award anytime soon, but I still like them.

I watched Fred settle on the top of my curtains. He squawked a couple of times, shook his wings, and quieted down.

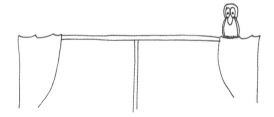

Then I fell asleep on the last partially normal night of my life.

CHAPTER 3

AN UNEXPECTED VISITOR

I'm not a morning person—mornings are too cold
and too quiet. I think the perfect way to start the
day is to roll out of bed once the sun has warmed
things up, eat a bunch of pancakes, and play video
games while my sister does my chores.

But this morning—way too early—Tuffin woke me up, and all because he wanted me to see a bug. I told him to leave me alone at least twenty times before I reluctantly got up. I had a quick glass of chocolate milk from the kitchen and followed Tuffin out front. He was talking about some bug and led me to an overturned bucket with a stain on it. He kept pointing at it and saying . . .

I couldn't really understand what he was saying, so I just nodded. He got mad that I was nodding and started to scream. Unluckily for me, Janae Welt was out front with her friends who had slept over, and they saw me. It was then that I remembered I was wearing what I had slept in: a huge old concert T-shirt of my dad's. Plus, my hair was a mess, I had a chocolate milk mustache, Tuffin was wailing, and Puck was chewing on an old sock.

I ran back inside as Janae and her friends laughed. It was not my proudest moment. I guess I was hoping to make a better impression.

I don't know why, but Janae and I had a rather complicated relationship. When we were seven, we were best friends.

When we were nine, we were disgusted with each other.

At eleven, we ignored each other.

But ever since the start of the school year, I wondered what it might *be* like to be friends with

her again. Now I had blown my chance by being seen in a big sloppy T-shirt with a drippy milk mustache.

I stormed back into my room and slammed the door. I changed into some of the clean clothes in my dresser, mumbling to myself about girls. I was just about to pinky swear to myself that I would never leave the house again when I heard a knock coming from the inside of my closet.

I figured some of the junk I had shoved in my closet was just settling, so I ignored the noise until there was a second knock. The hairs on the back of my neck stood up.

I stepped over to my closet. As usual, Beardy was smiling at me, but now it looked like he was also winking.

I reached out and touched the doorknob. It was kind of warm, and when I tried to turn the knob, it wouldn't budge. I twisted it the other way—nothing. I leaned my ear against the door and listened. I could hear a weird gurgling noise. I jumped back and stumbled over my bed and into the corner of my room. Libby walked by my door and saw me in the corner, hiding behind my bed and rocking.

THERE ARE NO SUCH THINGS AS GHOSTS.

I told her there was something in my closet.

WELL, I HOPE IT EATS YOU.

I asked Libby nicely to check for me, and she answered not nicely, telling me she wasn't going to fall for any tricks.

When I called for Tuffin to help, he didn't answer. I figured he was still out front pointing at the stain on the bucket. I called out for my dad, but he was in his room listening to the TV so loud that he couldn't hear me. I was about to call for my mother when Trevor popped up outside my window and knocked.

I jumped up from behind the bed and opened the window. Trevor climbed in and fell to the floor as I quickly closed my bedroom door. My mother hates the fact that most of my friends come in through my first-floor window. She likes to know exactly who's in the house at all times. I think she suspects that I will sneak in some really bad stuff.

Trevor was having a tizzy because his mom was making him babysit his cousin later. I couldn't really blame him for being mad. I mean, his cousin was a tiny, whiny troublemaker. His name was Copeland, and the one time I met him, he kicked me in the shin, called me fat, and told me that the only way he WOULDN'T tell everyone that I had hit him was if I gave him a dollar. I should have given him the dollar, because he screamed and cried—and Trevor's mom banished me from their house for a month.

I told Trevor that I was sorry for him having to babysit, but that I had a bigger problem. When he asked me what my "bigger problem" was, it sounded kind of lame coming out of my mouth.

MY CLOSET
KNOCKED
AT ME!

I told him that I couldn't open my closet door and that there was some sort of gurgling noise coming from inside. Trevor laughed at me and walked over to my closet. He tried to turn the knob, but it wouldn't open for him either. He put his ear to the door, but he couldn't hear anything. Trevor told me that I should probably get my hearing checked and turned toward the window to leave. That was when we both heard a . . .

CLICK!

The closet door squeaked open about an inch by itself. Both Trevor and I dove back behind my bed.

The closet door began to open wider. It was so heavy, I knew there was no way it could just drift open. The hinges squealed like a rusty iron pig.

Trevor pulled the pillow from my bed and stuck it over his face as I stared at the closet. I wanted to look away—actually, I wanted to crawl under my bed and call for my mom. But my body stayed right where it was, and my eyes were focused on my closet. Then the door flew open.

I grabbed my baseball bat as Trevor pulled the pillow off his head and screamed like a girl. The creature grunted, and Trevor dashed out the window faster than I thought possible. I gulped. I was alone with the thing from the closet.

It stared at me and groaned. I stood up slowly and took a really good look. After a couple of seconds, I dropped my bat and breathed in deeply. I would have been terrified if not for its size and smile.

The creature was a small, weird man who came up to just above my waist. He looked like two different people who had been smashed together. He wore a top hat and had a cane in one hand.

I rubbed my eyes and took another deep breath. I thought about running away like Trevor, but instead I sat down on the edge of my bed and tried to figure out what was happening. The little guy kept smiling. After staring for a few moments, I decided to poke him with a stick to see if he was real. He just laughed and batted the stick away. Next, I carefully grabbed his face and pulled.

This wasn't some kid in a mask. I thought maybe I was sick and hallucinating, but everything else looked normal.

The little creature began to pound the wall with his right hand. He started to sing a weird song and dance on his right foot. It was almost as if he was trying to impress me.

OMPAH, UMPAH, DOCTOR, URRG! OMPAH, DUHH, SCIENCE...

I was impressed, though I'm not sure whether it was a positive or negative impression.

I can't really explain what happened next. My head began to feel light. I mean, it could have been because I had only half a glass of chocolate milk to drink all morning. Or maybe it was because I was still tired, or that the day seemed warm. Or maybe it was because something otherworldly had just come out of my closet. I'm not proud of it, but for some reason I don't fully understand, I passed out.

CHAPTER 4

THE THING

When I woke up, it was eleven
thirty. My head hurt, and
everything was quiet. I rubbed
my eyes and looked around.

I was the only one in my room.
My window was open, so I closed it
and then walked to my closet.
Beardy was smiling, and when I tried to open the
closet door, it wouldn't budge. I laughed at myself—
maybe I had dreamt the whole thing. I combed my

hair and went out to the kitchen to get something
to eat.

Tuffin was in the kitchen sink. My little brother's
afraid of our pool out back, so he uses the big
kitchen sink to take a swim. He was playing an
imaginary game of Marco Polo with himself. He
always keeps one eye open and one eye closed so
that he can hide and find himself at the same time.

Libby was on the phone, talking to a boy named
Paul. I could tell his name was Paul because every
fourth word she said was *Paul*, followed by a giggle.

I plugged my ears so I could avoid hearing their conversation. My mom was sitting at the dining room table, doing bills and grumbling about how much food we all ate. I made the problem worse by getting some meat from the fridge and making myself a ham and peanut butter sandwich.

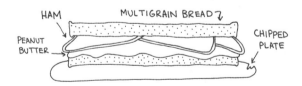

After I ate it, I began to feel better. I couldn't believe I had had such a crazy dream. As I was

swallowing my final bite, the doorbell rang. I ran
to get it, and when I opened the door, there was
Trevor, looking as pale as a sheet.

I saw something small dart back behind Trevor.
Apparently I hadn't been dreaming. I pointed at the
creature as he ran into the bushes and disappeared.
Trevor yelped as I quickly stepped outside and
closed the door behind me. The small guy dashed
out of the bushes and headed for the dirt field
where Aaron and Rourk were digging a big hole.

It was actually a community hole. All of us had been working on it for weeks. I started it one afternoon when I was bored. I figured I would dig a huge hole and then throw a party.

It was kind of fun at first, but then something hit me:

So I gave up on the hole, but Aaron and Rourk had kept at it in their free time, which they *seemed* to have a lot of. And now the creature from my closet was running right for the pit. I ran after him, but he jumped over the pile of dirt screaming and fell down into the abyss.

Rourk scrambled out, swearing like he was being attacked. It's no secret that Rourk likes to swear—it's one of the reasons why my parents don't like me hanging around him. He picks up words from his older brother. But I don't think he gets them right—half the time I can't tell if he's swearing or just making words up.

We all gathered around the hole, looking down at the thing in the bottom.

Hold on a second.

I should point out that I'm not one of those kids who has a ton of self-confidence. I don't walk into a crowded room and say things like . . .

I'm not always happy with how I look, my teeth are a bit crooked, I've never kissed a girl, unless you're talking about the old lady down the street, who I had to hug and kiss after she gave me a really rotten birthday present.

I'm not the greatest at sports. In fact, last year, when our soccer team was in the finals, I mistakenly reached up and caught the ball with my hands when I wasn't the goalie. I don't know why I did it—it was just a reflex. But the other team got a penalty kick, and they won the game. Afterward everyone kept patting me on the back really hard and congratulating me. I think they were being sarcastic.

Probably the most embarrassing thing about me is that I collect Thumb Buddies. When I was seven, Thumb Buddies were all the rage—fancy tiny pushpins decorated like characters.

THUMB BUDDIES

QUACK-TACK BRAD PAULA-PIN THUMB-PER POKE-KIN

COLLECT THEM ALL

THUMBTACKS OF FUN*

* ACTUAL FUN NOT INCLUDED

ARE YOUR THUMBS READY?

They were only popular for a short while, and after some kid in Texas poked himself one too many times, they stopped selling them. I should have grown out of it, but I kept collecting. I now have over five hundred different Thumb Buddies. I buy most of them on eBay, and once a year, they have a convention where other collectors meet and sell them.

Not even Trevor knows I still collect them—which is a good thing, seeing how even he might pick on me if he knew. It's an embarrassing secret, but I'm sure there are kids with worse ones.

Nope, I'm a pretty average kid. My grades aren't anything to brag about, my sister calls me a dork, I can't sing, and I can't play the piano with my rear like that one genius kid, Todd, who lives down the street.

I guess I'm a nobody, but I don't think I mind. I'm not the first person people think of, but I'm probably not the last. I'm kind of like a backup singer in the song of life. But lately my life has been cracking. If I close my eyes, I can see little lines of light, as if parts of me are falling away. My dad calls it . . .

Which I think is one of the most stupid-sounding words in the English language. Why can't it be called something less embarrassing like...

Anyway, my life was already beginning to feel a little different, and now this was happening?

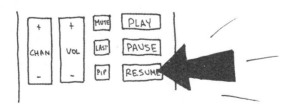

I looked down in the hole and felt sorry for the creature. He was kind of singing and crying, and I knew that if I pulled him out, my life was going to be changed forever.

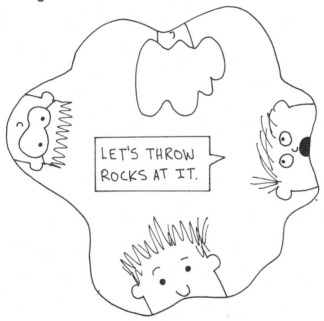

LET'S THROW ROCKS AT IT.

I pushed Rourk back, got down on my knees, and reached out. The small thing looked at my hand and smiled. I pulled him up and set him on the ground. Rourk and Aaron were having a fit, but I told them he was just a new toy my dad was testing out. I picked him up, put him under my arm, and marched home.

I walked back to my room and set the bundle on my bed. He smiled and started to sing softly. Some of his skin was greenish, and some was really pale. When I asked where he had come from, he just pointed at my closet. But when I tried to open my closet door, it was still locked tight.

The creature started to talk to himself. I was about to check my temperature when Trevor came tumbling in through the window.

Trevor stood by me while the little guy rambled. The thing was saying "gold" repeatedly and calling out for a doctor.

MAYBE HE'S SICK.

Both of us just stood there staring. Trevor suggested we feed him something, but I was afraid he would grow bigger if we did.

I couldn't tell my mom and dad. They would only ask where he came from and then discover how many things I had shoved into my closet, and that would be the end of my getting to do anything fun ever again.

So I did the only responsible thing I could think of. I closed my bedroom door, tucked the creature into my bed, and went out the window to be with my friends. I needed some time to think. I was hoping the little guy would just go to sleep and things would smooth out by themselves. I guess I'm just a hopeful person—hopeful but not incredibly smart.

CHAPTER 5

DRIVEN TO MADNESS

Being outside with my friends didn't help me feel much better. My stomach was tightening, and there was a thick layer of sweat on my forehead. Something baffling had come out of my closet, and that something was now sleeping in my bed.

SOMEBODY'S BEEN SLEEPING IN MY BED, AND SHE'S STILL THERE.

So I sat in the middle of the rock island beneath the palm trees and chewed my nails while trying to act normal. Jack said I looked like a . . .

Trevor wasn't looking much better than me. He had always been horrible at keeping secrets. Once, when I broke Janae's front window with a bowling ball, Trevor promised to not tell a soul. It was an accident, anyway. I never thought the bowling ball would actually go that far. Ten minutes into the investigation, Trevor cracked and spilled the secret. He even showed Janae's parents the plans for the catapult I had built and used.

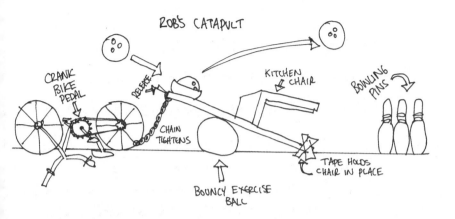

ROB'S CATAPULT

CRANK BIKE PEDAL

RELEASE

CHAIN TIGHTENS

KITCHEN CHAIR

BOWLING PINS

TAPE HOLDS CHAIR IN PLACE

BOUNCY EXERCISE BALL

Now Trevor was standing by me, shaking like a leaf.

And when Aaron and Rourk asked if they could see the big doll my dad had, I thought Trevor was going to pass out. I told them it had been deflated and packed away.

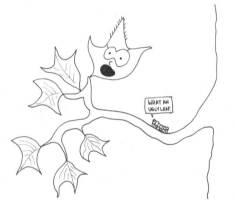

WHAT AN UGLY LEAF.

STORAGE

Mr. Pang came out of his awful house and put some garbage in his trash can on the curb. He looked at us with his old eyes and yelled something.

FLIBBERTIGIBBETS!

As soon as Mr. Pang went back inside, I dared Aaron to go see what he had thrown away. Aaron made up some lame excuse as to why he couldn't.

I'M ALLERGIC TO TRASH.

Rourk said he wouldn't do it because he used to have asthma. Teddy couldn't do it because he had just put on cologne, and he didn't want to ruin his smell. Trevor was still shaking like a leaf, so that left only Jack for me to dare. Jack said he would do it for a dollar. I gave him ninety-three cents, and he slunk across the street and up to the trash can. He looked both ways and then fake coughed while knocking the lid off.

COUGH!

Jack looked in and screamed. He ran back to us and told us there was a hand in the can.

HE'S BUILDING FRANKENSTEIN!

Teddy pointed out that
if Mr. Pang was building
Frankenstein, there wouldn't be a
hand in the trash because he would
need it. Jack argued that maybe the
hand didn't fit right, so they threw it away. I had
never seen a hand separated from its arm, and I
was kind of surprised when my feet started walking
across the street and toward the trash can. I
peeked over the edge.

UM...

There was no hand. I pulled out the object that
Jack must have mistaken for a hand.

It was at that moment that Janae's mother looked up from doing yard work across the street and saw me digging through Mr. Pang's trash. I would have waved at her, but there was a banana peel stuck to my hand.

Janae's mom shook her head and went inside. As I watched her go, I could see a small string of smoke coming out of my kitchen window. I told my friends I felt sick and needed to puke. Then I quickly ran across the street and into my house.

There was no smoke in the hallway, and the rest of the house looked normal. I moved into the kitchen. Tuffin was sitting on the counter, drying himself off with two oven mitts. He said something about strangers and pointed. There in front of the oven, standing on a chair, was the small thing I had tucked in my bed earlier. He was holding a large frying pan with a half-melted plastic bottle of chocolate syrup in it.

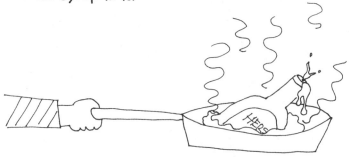

The kitchen was kind of smoky, but luckily the window was open and most of the smoke was drifting out. The creature's right side was dancing about while other bits of his left side were trying to get things under control.

I grabbed the pan and threw it into the sink. The water made the hot pan hiss and freaked the small guy out even more. He screamed and looked at me as if I were a mad scientist threatening to end his life. I smiled and stepped closer to him. He looked at the ground and then, with one great thrust, he moved across the room toward the wall. I thought the wall would stop him, but he busted through it and out into the garage.

Bits of wood and wallboard burst all over as Tuffin clapped and Puck began to bark. My mother got up off the couch and worked her way into the kitchen. I have to admit, it looked pretty bad.

Instead of taking the time to explain, I dropped to my knees and crawled out through the hole. My mom hollered after me as I fled.

The garage was dark, but I could hear someone banging on the garage door and screaming to get out.

I ran toward the noise. I reached out to grab at the thing, but he growled and dashed beneath my legs like a cat. I turned to go after him and he dashed back, causing me to lose my footing and stumble headfirst into the wall. My head slammed into the garage door opener. Ouch! I could see entire galaxies.

The garage door lifted open, but I was too dizzy to stop him from running.

I stood up and ran awkwardly after him. When I got out of the garage, I stopped and held my hand up over my eyes. I couldn't see him anywhere. I did, however, notice Janae walking to her car with her mother. I thought about smiling and waving, but they were looking the other way. Besides, I spotted my small visitor. He was standing beneath one of Janae's trees and rocking nervously.

Janae opened the car door on her side and turned to say something to her mother. At that very moment, the little thing made a break for it. He jumped from the trees, slipped behind Janae, and got into her car. He slid into the backseat without her seeing him. My jaw dropped.

Janae's mother got into the car as Janae climbed in and shut the passenger-side door. I couldn't move—my feet were frozen like Popsicles.

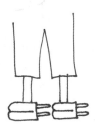

The vehicle backed out of the driveway and then stopped for a second before beginning to move forward. My feet finally thawed.

I ran down my driveway, screaming and waving, but it was too late. They couldn't hear me. I stared at the back of the car as it disappeared. I could feel my heart slip into my gut.

Trevor ran up to me, breathing hard. He waved a friendly wave at the car, and I hit him in the shoulder. We had to act quickly. I didn't know what to do, but I had a feeling that if we didn't do something, bad things were about to happen.

CHAPTER 6

SEARCHING

I had no idea where to look for Janae and the
little guy that had come from my closet. I mean,
the world's a pretty big place, and they could have
gone anywhere.

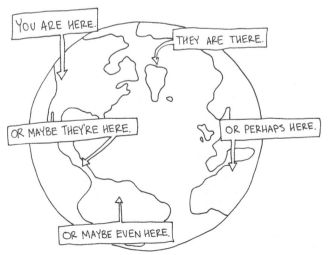

I rang the doorbell at Janae's house to see if somebody might know where they went, but nobody answered. I could see Janae's older sister, Lisa, peeking out at us from behind a slit in the curtains. Lisa was four years older than me, and we had never really gotten along. At first she tolerated me, but after what happened last year at the water park, she no longer even acknowledged me. I could be dying on the street with an arrow in my arm, my hair on fire, a knife in my leg, and a dog biting me, and she would skip right on by, singing.

DING-DONG, THE DORK IS GONE.

It wasn't like the water park incident was all *my* fault. Lisa was standing next to the lifeguards, making what she thought were pretty faces at one of them, when I came walking down the stairs, holding an ice cream cone.

SPILLED
SUNTAN
LOTION

I didn't mean to slip, but someone had spilled suntan lotion right where I was stepping. When I came crashing down, I landed on Lisa. I crammed my ice cream into her weird-shaped face, and it slid down the front of her. She screamed louder than a monkey singing opera.

FIGARO
FIGARO
FIGARO!!

In my opinion, I should have been the one screaming. I lost my ice cream and fell down in front of everyone. The only thing that happened to her was that her flirting was interrupted. Oh, and she might have badly twisted her ankle when she fell backward. Big deal, so she had to wear a foot brace for two months and use crutches, crutches she would smack me with whenever I got near her. Now Lisa was peering out of the curtains and pretending not to see us.

As tempting as Trevor's suggestion was, there was no way I was going to make things worse with Janae and her family. So we got our bikes and went to search for them. Trevor had to ride his sister's bike because the chain on his was broken.

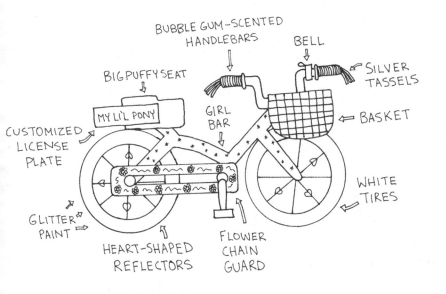

BUBBLE GUM-SCENTED HANDLEBARS

BELL

SILVER TASSELS

BIG PUFFY SEAT

GIRL BAR

BASKET

CUSTOMIZED LICENSE PLATE

MY LI'L PONY

WHITE TIRES

GLITTER PAINT

HEART-SHAPED REFLECTORS

FLOWER CHAIN GUARD

We couldn't decide where to look for Janae and the creature. Trevor suggested that we go to the places girls always go. I told him he would know what those places were, seeing how he was riding a girl's bike. So we rode to all the places we thought a girl might hang out.

They weren't at the mall. They weren't at the bakery, the hair salon, or the nail salon. They weren't in the grocery store, flipping through the latest issue of *Teenish Dreams.*

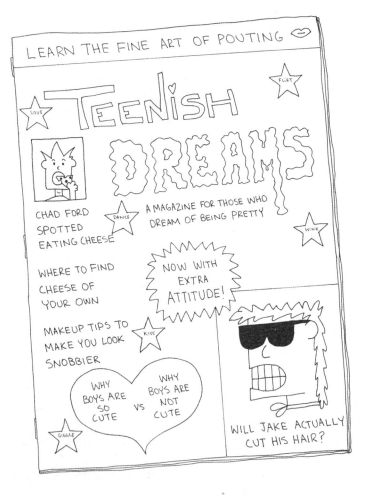

LOVE

FLIRT

TEENISH DREAMS

CHAD FORD SPOTTED EATING CHEESE

DANCE

A MAGAZINE FOR THOSE WHO DREAM OF BEING PRETTY

WINK

WHERE TO FIND CHEESE OF YOUR OWN

NOW WITH EXTRA ATTITUDE!

MAKEUP TIPS TO MAKE YOU LOOK SNOBBIER

KISS

WHY BOYS ARE SO CUTE

VS

WHY BOYS ARE NOT CUTE

GIGGLE

WILL JAKE ACTUALLY CUT HIS HAIR?

They weren't buying ribbons at the ribbon store or lip gloss at Target. They weren't in any of the spots that we thought a girl might go. Trevor suggested we check the fancy underwear store, but I refused to step inside.

Since we were exhausted and out of ideas, we decided to go home and regroup. While we were pedaling back, we finally spotted Janae's mom's car. It was in the parking lot of the public library. I had completely forgotten that girls like books.

We carefully checked her car for any sign of the little guy. He wasn't in there. The only things we saw were a couple of CDs and an opened bag of Cheetos. We biked around the library searching the bushes and looking in the trees. I told Trevor that we needed to go into the library, but we couldn't because I didn't have a license.

He laughed at me for two minutes and asked me when was the last time I went to the library. I was actually embarrassed to admit that it was when I was seven and came for a "Bookday" party for Jack. It was like a birthday party, but the only gifts you got were books. So it was a pretty big rip for Jack. He acted as if he liked it, but I could tell by the way he kept saying...

... that he was just being polite. And every time his dad handed him a present to open, his dad shook it and said the same lame joke over and over:

I guess adults just have a different sense of humor than kids.

Trevor informed me that you didn't need a license to go into the library, just to check out books. I told Trevor that I knew that, and that I'd just gotten mixed up.

The inside of the library was huge. There was a big atrium in the center with a large tree and a small fishpond. Around the atrium was a spiral staircase. A lady with a crooked wig and big glasses was sitting at a desk near the front door. Her name tag said . . .

HELLO, MY NAME IS...

SHELLEY

She asked if she could help us and then licked her dry lips and handed us a bookmark.

READING MAKES
ME
WHISTLE

GOOD BOOK.

Trevor started to ask her if she had seen a short guy with a hat and some greenish skin. Luckily I elbowed him before he got his whole question out. The woman licked her lips again and stared at us. It was then that I spotted some tiny wet footprints on the floor.

I pointed to the footprints and Trevor

told the lady that we just wanted to look at the fishpond. She warned us not to throw anything at the fish and then handed us another bookmark.

We followed the tiny footprints until they ended near the poetry section.

MAYBE HE LIKES POETRY.

I was about to call Trevor dumb when Janae came walking around the corner. She saw me and actually smiled. She then stopped right in front of me. I tried to say something cool.

SO YOU'RE AT THE LIBRARY.

It wasn't the smoothest thing to say, but she nodded. I asked her who she had come with, and she said her mother. Then I asked if she had come with anyone else, and she said no. I asked her if she was absolutely positive that she hadn't come with anyone else, and she said yes. But when I asked her . . .

IS THERE ANY WAY YOU DID ACCIDENTALLY COME WITH SOMEONE ELSE BUT THAT YOU DIDN'T KNOW IT AT FIRST AND THEN YOU FOUND OUT WHEN YOU GOT TO THE LIBRARY AND HE JUMPED OUT OF YOUR CAR WITHOUT YOU BEING ABLE TO STOP HIM OR TALK TO HIM?

Janae took a couple of steps back. Trevor sort of saved things by quickly asking her a normal question about the books she was checking out. Janae said she was getting some dramatic poems so she could pick one to perform at the school assembly coming up in a few weeks. When she asked us what we were doing there, I choked. Maybe it was because I was worried about the little guy we had lost. Maybe it was because Janae made me nervous and I had already said some dumb things. I don't know what it was, but my mouth kept running and I said the stupidest thing ever.

I'M DOING SOMETHING DRAMATIC ALSO.

LIKE A POEM?

YEAH, THAT'S IT. I'M DOING A POEM AT THE ASSEMBLY.

Janae seemed pleased. She smiled again and told me how surprised she was. She even offered to practice with me and help me memorize my poem if I wanted. I shook my head, wondering what a dramatic poem really was and wishing that my dumb mouth would stop making a fool out of me. I was going to try to straighten things out, but I spotted something small dashing past the end of the shelves. I told Janae that Trevor and I needed to go to the bathroom and left.

Trevor also saw the mini shadow. We ran down a row of bookshelves as quietly as possible. Trevor moved off to the side and slipped through the science fiction section as I moved through fantasy.

The tiny dark outline dashed across our path. I ran through the fiction section, and we trapped the thing in an empty chair. Luckily there was nobody else around. The little guy appeared more concerned than scared. He was shaking, and his eyes looked us up and down. I was about to wrap my arms around him and pick him up when he spoke.

Trevor and I both stepped back. I had never heard the creature say anything that made this much sense. But who was Charlie? After shaking off the shock of hearing him speak an understandable sentence, I told him our real names and that he needed to come with us. He asked a second question.

WHO AM I?

It wasn't easy to answer. I picked him up and set him on one of the shelves so that I could look at him eye to eye. He sighed and called me friend. I asked him if he remembered anything about himself, and he answered by saying that one half of him remembered working in a factory, but the other half of him felt confused and lonely and out of place. When I asked him what kind of factory, he said all he could remember was that there was lots of chocolate. Trevor started dancing around like he really did need to use the bathroom.

Trevor ran off, and I picked up the little thing and told him to keep quiet. He seemed to understand. He grunted and shut his mouth. By the time we caught up with Trevor, he had found what he was looking for. It was the book *Charlie and the Chocolate Factory*. Trevor was jumping up and down. He started talking about how the little guy was a mix of Willy Wonka and Frankenstein.

That made me think of Frank-n-Stick.

Apparently Trevor had no idea who Frank-n-Stick

was.

FRANK-N-STICK

Trevor insisted that the creature from my closet

was kind of a half Willy Wonka and half a wee

version of Dr. Frankenstein's monster.

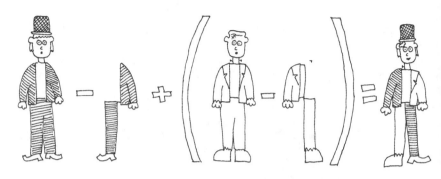

I informed Trevor that Frankenstein was the name of the creature, but Trevor was pretty sure that Frankenstein was actually the man who had made the monster. I told him I had seen the cartoon and he was wrong. I even bet him five bucks that I was right.

AND I'M CALLING HIM WONKENSTEIN.

Trevor was okay with that, but he said we should check out the book *Charlie and the Chocolate Factory*. Unfortunately, he didn't have a library card either. We also had Wonkenstein with us. There was no way we could get one with him *babbling*.

I CAN STAY QUIET.

Wonkenstein seemed sincere, so we took him and stood in line to get library cards. When we got to the front of the line, the lady commented on what an interesting and realistic-looking doll I had. I tried to explain that it wasn't a doll, it was a ventriloquist dummy. Unfortunately, Janae was walking by at just the same moment.

DO YOU ALWAYS BRING YOUR TOYS WITH YOU TO THE LIBRARY?

ONLY SOMETIMES.

Trevor got a library card, and we checked out the book and hurried away. Wonkenstein was excellent at staying quiet. The Willy Wonka part of him seemed to understand how important it was, while the monster part of him was too confused to act out.

We sat Wonk in Trevor's bike basket and rode home as fast as we could. We cut through the golf course and raced down the hill behind the school. Trevor got going too fast, and while trying to straighten out, he accidentally swerved and hit a curb. Wonkenstein went flying over a fence. His arms were flailing as he screamed . . .

SCIENCE!!

COMMUNITY
GUM
CHEWING
CONTEST
FEBRUARY 1ST

BRING YOUR OWN GUM
MAY THE BEST
JAWS WIN!

TEDDY
OS
LIBBY

Then we heard him splash down in someone's backyard pool. I leapt off my bike and climbed over the fence as fast as I could. Wonkenstein was thrashing around in the water. I jumped in to try to save him, but he was hysterical. He kept scratching at my head and pulling my hair. He stuck one of his tiny thumbs in my right eye and kicked me in the stomach. Trevor got the skimmer from the side of the pool and tried to fish us out, but that just made things worse.

I finally got hold of an inner tube and shoved it over him like a single handcuff. It bound Wonk's arms, and he screamed while floating in the water. Eventually he calmed down and took a deep breath.

He was fine—a little wet but fine. I, on the other hand, was not. I was missing a big chunk of hair, I had a black eye, and my shirt was ripped.

The owner of the pool came out of his house and chased us off with a mop.

By the time we got to my house and crawled in the window, we were exhausted. I was just about to breathe a huge sigh of relief when someone knocked loudly and forcefully on my bedroom door.

KNOCK!

CHAPTER 7

FORCING THINGS

I'm an expert at recognizing my family's knocks. If it's low down on the door and sounds like someone is slapping a dead fish against it, it's Tuffin.

FLOP, FLOP!

If it's to the side and just above the doorknob with an impatient rapping sound, it's Libby. If it's right in the center and only two knocks, it's my mom. If it's

three hard knocks, it's my mom and she's mad. And
if it is a friendly

then I know for sure it's my dad. The rarest knock
is the forceful, loud knock my father executes when
he's upset—and that was the knock I had just
heard.

   Trevor looked at the window, but it was too late
to escape. The doorknob turned, and my father
stepped in. We quickly threw a quilt over the
mumbling Wonkenstein.

 My dad was sporting his mean face, which didn't look much different from his happy face, except there was no smile.

He wanted to know who was responsible for almost burning down our kitchen and knocking a huge hole in the wall. Trevor glanced down at the floor and started shaking. I don't always have brilliant ideas right when I need them, but I did this time. I knew my dad would never get mad at a guest, so I pointed to the blanket-covered Wonkenstein.

HE'S NEW IN THE NEIGHBORHOOD.

My dad instantly cooled down. He pulled the blanket off Wonk. I thought we'd be busted for sure, but my dad barely flinched. He thought Wonkenstein was just a really small kid dressed oddly and with some green skin condition. My dad knelt on one knee and started to talk nicely to him.

DON'T BE SHY. I SAW A SHOW ON THE LOOKING CHANNEL ABOUT YOUR CONDITION.

I DON'T THINK HE SPEAKS ENGLISH.

My dad tried out his really poor Spanish that he hadn't spoken since his freshman year in high school. It was bad enough by itself, but it was even worse because he was mixing it with some of the French he hadn't spoken since his sophomore year.

My dad lectured Wonkenstein on how in our house we use doors, not walls, to leave. He then pulled me and Trevor aside and whispered something to us, acting like he was sharing some great secret.

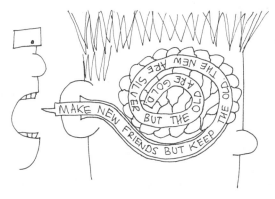

We thanked him for the advice and promised to help him patch up the wall. He seemed happy about that and left us.

As soon as my dad was gone, I tried to open my closet again. I was thinking that I could just put Wonkenstein back in there and everything would return to normal. But the closet door was still stuck tight. Even the knob wouldn't turn.

YOU NEED TO GET A HAMMER AND BUST IT OPEN.

I LOST MY DAD'S HAMMER. I'VE GOT A BUTTER KNIFE.

A BUTTER KNIFE'S NOT GOING TO DO IT.

HOW ABOUT A TOOTHBRUSH?

I'M WORRIED ABOUT YOU. I'LL GET A HAMMER FROM MY HOUSE.

Trevor jumped back out the window to go get a hammer. That left Wonkenstein and me alone in the room.

I wanted to tell him that more than a bit of me was confused, but I kept it to myself. I sat down on the floor, and Wonkenstein patted me on the right shoulder. I smiled at him, and he grunted loudly.

A few minutes later, Trevor climbed through the window carrying a huge hammer. I didn't know what to say while swinging a hammer, so I just yelled . . .

I whacked it against the doorknob, but nothing happened.

Then Jack showed up at the window.

Jack jumped through the window and was in the room before I could hide Wonkenstein. Jack looked at him.

Trevor and I began to spill our guts. We told Jack everything that had happened, and when we were done, Jack volunteered to keep Wonkenstein for the night.

It took me ten minutes to convince Jack that
Wonk was not a pet. But since Jack's parents were
working and his older brother, Harry, was taking
care of him, I thought it would be easier to hide
Wonkenstein at his house. Besides, he had a huge
closet with a door that actually opened. When I
tried to explain to Wonkenstein what was happening,
he looked at me and pointed toward Jack.

I considered warning him about some of Jack's less friendly traits, but I didn't want to make things worse.

As he was leaving, Wonkenstein handed me a small piece of candy.

I thanked him, and he patted me on the knee. Then they left me and Trevor alone. We began to speculate about what was going on. We even wrote a list of what we knew.

WHAT WE KNOW...

① HE CAME FROM THE CLOSET.

② PART OF HIM ACTS LIKE WILLY WONKA.

③ SOME OF HIS SKIN IS SORTA GREENISH.

④ HE HAS A CANE AND A HAT.

⑤ WE SHOULDN'T LEAVE HIM WITH JACK TOO LONG.

⑥ WILLY WONKA IS NOT JUST A MOVIE.

⑦ HE GRUNTS A LOT.

⑧ TREVOR RUNS AWAY WHEN HE'S SCARED.

⑨ MUSHROOMS ARE DISGUSTING.

Then we wrote down the things we didn't know.

WHAT WE DON'T KNOW...
① WHY HE CAME FROM THE CLOSET
② WHAT WE SHOULD FEED HIM
③ IF WE SHOULD KEEP HIM
④ WHAT TO DO WITH HIM WHILE WE'RE AT SCHOOL
⑤ IF WE ARE JUST DREAMING
⑥ IF WE SHOULD TELL OUR PARENTS
⑦ WHY GIRLS ARE SO CONFUSING
⑧ WHY SUGAR-FREE CANDY GIVES YOU GAS
⑨ WHY PEOPLE BOTHER MAKING LISTS

The lists didn't really help. We both knew that
the real answers were behind the closet door. My
closet was crammed with books and junk and
old laboratory supplies, but there had to be an
explanation for what was happening in there. I tried
the knob again, but it still wouldn't budge.

Trevor dashed off and was back in no time with a huge coil of rope. I guess his mom was expecting to tie up a really fat burglar. I took the rope and tied one end of it to my closet doorknob. I threw the rest out the window.

As we headed out into the front yard, Trevor kept asking what I was doing. I didn't answer him because

I wanted it to be a surprise. I tied the other end of the rope to my bike and then hopped on. I pedaled as hard and fast as I could.

The rope uncoiled quickly, but instead of yanking my closet open, it yanked my bike out from under me and sent me flying into the thick bushes on the rock island in the middle of the cul-de-sac.

I think Trevor was finally surprised. At least he acted that way as he helped pull me out of the bushes. I was pretty scraped up, but all my arms and legs worked. The closet, however, was still shut tight. I suggested that maybe Trevor should try riding the bike, but he wasn't willing. So we unhooked the rope from the bike and tied it to

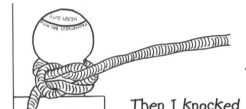

the back hitch of my neighbor Victor's truck. Then I knocked on Victor's door.

As expected, Victor tore out of his house and jumped into his truck. He peeled out and raced down the street. For a brief moment, the rope went taut and then . . .

The end whipped around my neighbor's mailbox and ripped it from the ground. Trevor and I just stood there as mail rained down.

I got hit in the eye by a furniture catalog, and Trevor got a phone bill down the back of his shirt. Plus, a small package thwacked me in the stomach. The one thing that didn't happen, however, was my closet door opening, which made my stomach feel worse than the package hitting me.

It was getting late, and Trevor started insisting he had to go home, so we agreed to meet in the morning before school.

I was going to go to Jack's house and check on Wonkenstein, but Tuffin came out holding a baseball bat and a jar of dill pickles.

PICKLE BALL?

I figured I had done enough things to make my family mad for one day, so I decided to spend time with Tuffin. It was a bad decision for two reasons: One, Tuffin wanted to play pickleball, and that ended up making a huge mess. And, two, at the same moment I was hitting a "dill-ble," things were getting a little sticky for Wonkenstein at Jack's house.

But I didn't know about that yet, so I finished my game with Tuffin and went in to read *Charlie and the Chocolate Factory.*

CHAPTER 8

TAFFY

I hate *being* woken up from a good dream. I mean,
it's a real letdown to *be* dreaming about hitting a
home run in the World Series one moment and then
just lying in your bed the next. But sometimes my
dreams get a little confusing, and waking up is
probably a good thing. I suppose that's why I wasn't
too bothered to be woken up while dreaming about
riding on a motorcycle and jumping over a large
mound of spaghetti. I was wearing a big hat, and

Janae was feeding me grapes while Jack was waving a Hey-There Kitty flag.

It was raining outside, so the thunder must have woken me up. I shifted on my bed, and my book fell to the floor. I had read a lot of *Charlie and the Chocolate Factory* before falling asleep, and my head was still filled with thoughts of candy and chocolate. I looked over at my clock.

VERY, VERY LATE O'CLOCK

I listened to the rain for a moment and then shut my eyes. As I felt myself beginning to drift off again, a steady wheezing noise started to fill my ears. My eyes flashed open once more.

Jack had come in through my window without permission. He put his hand over my mouth and begged me to stop screaming. I bit his palm and then had to beg him to stop screaming. Luckily, the heavy rain covered up most of the noise we were making. Once we had both calmed down and were breathing normally, I spoke.

WHERE'S WONKENSTEIN?

YOU MEAN TAFFY?

YOU NAMED HIM TAFFY?

WHAT? SOME OF HIS SKIN'S GREEN AND HE KEEPS TALKING ABOUT CANDY.

2112

I told Jack that the reason Wonk kept talking about candy was because half of him was Willy Wonka, the greatest candy maker in all of literature. Jack didn't seem that impressed, but he did manage to tell me that both halves had run away. I got out

of bed. Jack was holding a long wooden staff with
what looked like a flashlight attached with duct
tape to the end of it
and a fork taped to
that.

IT'S AN ASSAULT FLASHLIGHT.

I didn't have time to make fun
of him. I changed my clothes, and
we both climbed out my window and
ran to the rock island. Rain was
dropping in buckets, but the palm trees provided
some shelter. We huddled in the middle of the trees
and yelled at each other. Jack had no idea where
Wonk could have gone.

Jack explained how he had dressed Wonk up in one of his little sister's dance outfits and was training him to jump through a Hula-Hoop when Wonkenstein accidentally knocked over their fish tank. They saved the fish, but the water spilled into one of the light sockets and shorted out the electricity in their house.

Jack said when he lit a candle for light, the fire scared Wonkenstein and he bolted.

My brain whirled. Ever since Wonkenstein had first appeared, my solution was to simply get rid of him so I wouldn't get in trouble. But now I could see that probably wasn't the best strategy.

I shined Jack's assault flashlight around the island and into the falling rain. The night was dark, but most of the houses in the neighborhood had their front porch lights on. There were no cars out, and weak lightning flashed, followed by a dull thunder. I looked up and saw that one of the top-floor windows of the Awful House was glowing. I aimed the assault flashlight toward it. I wouldn't have paid too much attention to it if it hadn't been for the fuzzy shadow I could see in the bottom corner of the window.

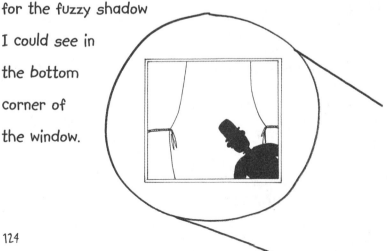

Wonk was in there! My stomach and heart began to beat each other up.

Jack and I crawled under some of the large bushes near the edge of the island and looked through the rain toward the Awful House. I saw Wonk's shadow move away from the window.

I thought of Mr. Pang and his large son, Ogre. I thought of all the stories we had made up about the Awful House.

My brain whirled again, and I knew there was no way I was going to get out of this. I had pushed the problem aside long enough. Don't get me wrong—I was pretty tempted just to run back to my house and bury myself in my bed and pretend this wasn't my trouble. But a small, nagging part of me kept poking me in the chest and demanding I do what was right.

So I scrambled out from beneath the bushes and bravely marched across the street.

All right, maybe I bravely crawled, but at least I was going in.

CHAPTER 9

LOCK YOUR DOORS

I crept around to the far side of the Awful House, past the creaking windmill and up to the back door. Jack had promised to keep watch outside and cover me with his assault flashlight. He also promised to alert the authorities if I wasn't back quickly. I knew he really wouldn't do that, so I made him at least promise to tell Trevor and then Trevor could wake my parents and they could get the police. I also knew it probably wouldn't go that smoothly.

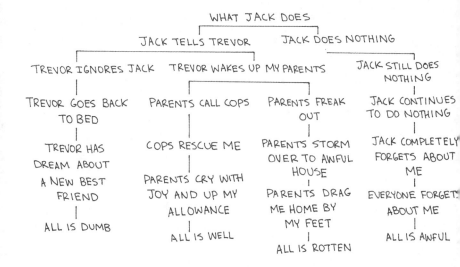

WHAT JACK DOES

JACK TELLS TREVOR — JACK DOES NOTHING

TREVOR IGNORES JACK — TREVOR WAKES UP MY PARENTS — JACK STILL DOES NOTHING

TREVOR GOES BACK TO BED — PARENTS CALL COPS — PARENTS FREAK OUT — JACK CONTINUES TO DO NOTHING

TREVOR HAS DREAM ABOUT A NEW BEST FRIEND — COPS RESCUE ME — PARENTS STORM OVER TO AWFUL HOUSE — JACK COMPLETELY FORGETS ABOUT ME

ALL IS DUMB — PARENTS CRY WITH JOY AND UP MY ALLOWANCE — PARENTS DRAG ME HOME BY MY FEET — EVERYONE FORGETS ABOUT ME

ALL IS WELL — ALL IS ROTTEN — ALL IS AWFUL

The Awful House looked even worse in the rain. I thought about just knocking on the door and asking to go in, but I knew Mr. Pang would never allow that. Besides, he was probably asleep, and waking him up seemed like a really bad idea. So I figured the smartest or dumbest thing to do was to just sneak up to the house and try to coax Wonkenstein out somehow.

I crawled through the tall, wet weeds and over to the weathered back porch. The steps creaked and whined as I climbed them.

I could see how Wonkenstein had gotten in. The back door was banging in the wind. It would open a few inches, slam shut, and then pop open again. I was actually disappointed. I had been sort of hoping the back door would be locked so that I could just leave.

I'M LOCKED. NOTHING TO SEE HERE. MOVE ALONG NOW.

That wasn't the case. The door blew open, and I slipped inside. I could see a light shining from down the hall, and I could hear a TV. The house was old, and the hallway wall was covered with a large mural of an underwater scene. It wasn't a very good painting. A big, mushy-looking whale with fat googly eyes was staring at me with his right peeper.

I could see some stairs going up to the second floor. I climbed them slowly while my mind kept whispering to me.

PSST, EARS. THIS IS A BAD IDEA.

WE'RE NOT LISTENING.

I reached the second floor and shuffled quietly in the direction of the window I had seen Wonkenstein standing near. I whispered as calmly as I could . . .

There was no reply.

I heard some knocking coming from a shadowy doorway. I tried to convince myself I was brave while moving into the room and looking around.

There was a soft light shining, and on the wall I could see a large mural of an African jungle.

There was also a wooden trunk at the end of a thin bed. While I was looking at the trunk, it suddenly shook. I was just about to turn around and run screaming from the house when the top of the trunk popped open and a small black shadow leapt toward me. I didn't react well. I fell backward as Wonkenstein smashed into me, and we both tumbled to the floor.

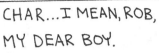

CHAR...I MEAN, ROB, MY DEAR BOY.

I tried to shush him, but he just kept grunting and telling me how marvelous it was to see me again. He was still wearing the dance costume and was covered in beads. I could hear Mr. Pang yelling something from down below—this was followed by the sound of footsteps thumping up the stairs. I had no time to really think things through. I ordered Wonkenstein to keep quiet and then used the mural to help us hide.

Mr. Pang stuck his head in and looked around for a few seconds. He grunted, blamed the noise on the rain, and walked back downstairs. I breathed out, and Wonkenstein smiled at me.

WHAT A MARVELOUS ADVENTURE.

YOU'RE NUTS.

He then began talking about how he loved nuts, so I had to put my hand over his mouth to keep him quiet.

When we finally made it downstairs and to the back door, I discovered that Mr. Pang had locked it. Plus, it wasn't the kind of lock you could just twist open from inside—it was the kind that needed a key. I moved along the wall to see if I could open a window, but all the windows had locks on them too. I kept hoping that Jack and Trevor would burst into the house with assault flashlights and rescue us.

DON'T MAKE A MOVE OR WE'LL SHINE ON YOU!

I glanced down the long hallway toward the sound of the TV and realized that the only way to get out was to go past Mr. Pang and through the front door. I held Wonkenstein's hand and we crept down the hall. When we got to the living room, I could see Mr. Pang sitting in a recliner next to a small table. He was wearing an old robe and staring at a huge TV. The volume was up really loud. I could see the remote in the front pocket of his robe and wondered why he didn't use it to turn the sound down.

I looked at Wonkenstein and put my finger to my lips. We stepped as carefully as we could along the wall, toward the front door. We were right behind Mr. Pang's chair when Wonkenstein noticed a small dish of hard candy on the little table.

Before I could stop him, Wonkenstein reached out and grabbed a piece. The dish rattled, and Mr. Pang jumped in his chair and spun around. I ducked down behind the chair, holding Wonkenstein as still as possible.

Mr. Pang looked around and shifted his chair
to have a better view of the hallway and room. By
moving his chair, he had unknowingly pinned us
against the wall. He sat back down and continued
to watch TV. We were trapped, and I couldn't think
of a single way to save us.

CHAPTER 10

SAVED BY CANDY

Luckily for us, I didn't have to think of anything.
Instead, I let the book I had been reading think for
me. I reached into my pocket and pulled out the
piece of candy that Wonkenstein had given me
earlier. Wonkenstein looked at it and smiled as I
asked . . .

WHAT DOES THIS DO?

Wonk shrugged, and his eyes widened. I knew the candy had to do something. After all, the candy in the book was anything but boring. I figured it would turn whoever ate it into a huge blueberry or make their hair grow. I was tempted to try it myself, but we needed a distraction. As quietly as I could, I unwrapped it and reached out from behind the chair. I placed the piece of candy on top of the pile in the candy dish. Not more than thirty seconds later, Mr. Pang picked it up and tossed it into his mouth.

He chewed, grunted a few times, and picked up another piece of candy. I was pretty disappointed— apparently the candy didn't do anything. Wonkenstein patted me on the knee and growled quietly. I knew we had to get out, but I couldn't see how. I considered waiting until Mr. Pang went to bed, but if he slept in his chair, that wouldn't work. I thought about pretending I had just wandered into the house while sleepwalking, and walking out, but I didn't think Mr. Pang would fall for it.

I was beginning to really worry when I heard a small yelp from the other side of the chair. I thought it was the TV, but then the chair began to shake. Wonkenstein started to panic. He kicked against the back of the chair and grunted loudly. The beads he was wearing rattled. I wanted to shut him up, but I was also concerned about what was happening to Mr. Pang. The chair was still shaking, and he was hollering. I pushed up and looked over the back of the chair. I don't know what I was expecting to see, but it wasn't this:

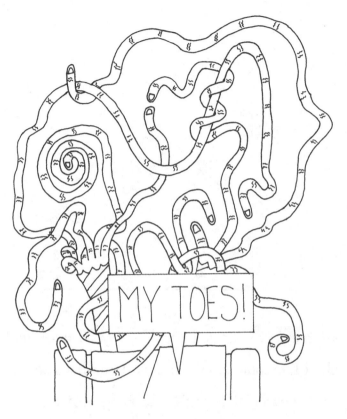

Mr. Pang's toes had burst out of his socks and were twisting and growing at an amazing rate. Some were coiling up in piles, and others were shooting up the fireplace or across the floor. I thought about running for the front door, but his right big toe and left pinky toe were blocking the way.

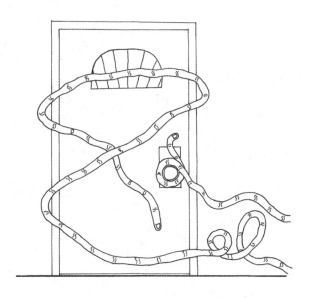

I tossed Wonkenstein up over my shoulder and pushed the chair away from us. I ran back down the hall and up the stairs. Mr. Pang spotted me and yelled . . .

SHAVE A COW!!

He might have actually yelled "STOP RIGHT NOW," but I couldn't tell for sure. I ran up the stairs as Mr. Pang tried to follow, dragging his long toes. He was pretty fast for an old guy.

I reached the top of the stairs and looked around. I could hear Mr. Pang climbing up behind me. Wonkenstein seemed to be enjoying it all because he kept laughing and grunting.

I was about to run into the room with the safari mural and try to hide again when I saw a door open. It had a KEEP OUT sign on it and a hand sticking out.

The hand gestured for me to come closer. I ignored the sign and took a step toward it. The door opened wider, and Wonkenstein and I were pulled in. I could hear the door shut behind me as I fell against a soft bed. I turned over quickly, thinking I might have to defend myself.

SHHHHHH...

It was Ogre. I could hear Mr. Pang thrashing outside the bedroom door. Ogre told us to stay put. He then went out into the hall and shut the door behind him. My heart was beating a million times per minute, and my forehead was sweaty.

Wonkenstein looked down at the outfit Jack had put on him. He pulled off the necklaces and squirmed out of the tutu. I was mad at Jack, but this was really all my fault. I knew better than to leave anything in Jack's care. One time a few years ago, I had let Jack borrow some of my Legos, and when I got them back, they were all melted together with a pair of Barbie legs and an old hairbrush.

Wonkenstein grunted. We could hear Ogre arguing with his dad in the hall. A few minutes later, Ogre came into the room and shut the door behind him. He told us his dad had really long toes, but that they were shrinking back. I tried to look cool and as if I had no idea how that had happened.

Ogre then said that his dad had seen me and was going to call the police. When I asked Ogre why he was helping us, he just shrugged.

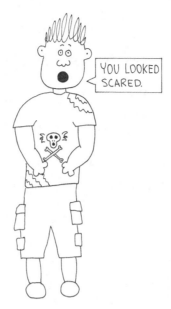

I was going to argue that point, but since it was true, I let it go.

Ogre unlocked his bedroom window and helped Wonkenstein and me out and into the wet tree branches. The rain was beginning to let up. I begged Ogre to not tell anyone about Wonkenstein.

I shinnied down the wet tree with Wonkenstein sitting on my shoulders and holding on to my head. Rain sprayed me in the face as I ran home. When I got back to my house, I crawled through my window. I had barely shoved Wonk beneath the bed and jumped under my covers when my bedroom door burst open. My parents were standing there, and they didn't look happy. Of course, my dad never really looks happy without his glasses on.

GUESS WHO DOESN'T ENJOY GETTING PHONE CALLS AT MIDNIGHT?

I'LL GUESS FOR YOU-US!

Apparently they had gotten a call from Mr. Pang, and now they wanted some answers. I tried to tell them that I had *been* in my room all night, but the fact that I was soaking wet sort of blew my cover.

A police car pulled up to our house, and two cops came in to talk to me. I was going to spill the beans about everything, but the cop just started talking, and I knew it was rude to interrupt.

I felt pretty happy about how it turned out. But when my father and I accompanied the cops out to their car, I noticed Janae and her mom looking out of their front window. Janae's mom was shaking her head.

Sometimes adults can be a little judgmental.

CHAPTER 11

FIZZY

My parents weren't quite as quick to let me off
the hook as the cops were. My mom sent me to
my room and promised she would think of a proper
punishment for me in the morning. I could see the
ideas already forming in her head.

I was so pumped up from my adventure that I couldn't fall asleep. So I finished the rest of *Charlie and the Chocolate Factory* while Wonkenstein slept at the foot of my bed. I had never read so fast or so much, but I wanted answers.

Still, I was pretty tired in the morning. I fell asleep on the bus and started to snore. Teddy made the situation even worse by sticking straws in my nose and trash in my hair.

When I got to school, the bus driver woke me up and I hefted my backpack onto my shoulders. I hadn't wanted to leave Wonkenstein at home, so I had tucked him in my backpack. I had also put a bottle of soda and a bunch of fruit snacks in there to keep him happy during the long school day.

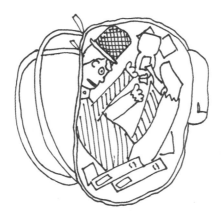

Right after first period, I went to the school library and checked out the book *Frankenstein*. As I was coming out of the library, I bumped into Jack. I thanked him for not helping me last night, and he didn't even say sorry. He told me that he went straight home after I had gone into the Awful

House. When I reminded him that I COULD HAVE
DIED, he repeated what his dad always says to us.

COULD HAVES
TURN TO
SHOULD HAVES.

I'd never understood what that meant, so I just
punched Jack in the right shoulder and walked away.

I was both surprised and happy about how well
Wonkenstein did keeping quiet in my backpack.
Sadly, that changed during lunch. I had just walked
up to Janae to explain what she and her mom had
seen last night. But before I could tell her, she
began talking about the dramatic poetry contest

and how the performance would be in two weeks. She also informed me that she had already gone to the trouble of signing me up. Janae then asked me if I was going to be nervous, and when I opened my mouth to speak, Wonkenstein let it fly. I'm not sure what it was. Maybe it was the soda I had given him, or all the jostling in my backpack. Either way, he burped louder and longer than I had ever heard anyone burp before. I was horrified, but the only thing I could do was stand there with my mouth hanging open and try to make it look like it was me.

I could have been wrong, but it looked like Janae was going to cry. She dropped her apple and ran out of the lunchroom before I could explain. Rourk complimented me on my burp while Mrs. Wetting grabbed me by the ear and dragged me to the principal's office.

Principal Smelt has been the principal of Joseph P. Softrock Middle School for twenty years. He's a nice guy, and he plays the pan flute—which is probably not what you think it is.

REAL PAN FLUTE

BLOW HERE

He also has a singing group that's made up of him and one other old guy who shakes a tambourine and harmonizes. They call themselves Leftover Angst, which is a name I don't understand. I understand *leftover*, but *angst* is a new word for me. If I had to guess, I bet it means "old people who are trying to act young but not having much success at it."

Principal Smelt and his band love to play songs at our assemblies. It doesn't matter what the assembly's theme is, he seems to always have an original song that fits. Once when we had a speaker come and talk to us about hygiene and using deodorant and stuff, Principal Smelt managed to have a song about that as well.

I thought that was the most embarrassing song I had ever heard, but then when me and Trevor were at the mall once, we saw Principal Smelt and his band in front of Sears, singing about underwear on sale.

Unfortunately, Principal Smelt wasn't in a singing mood. He lectured me about manners and made me promise to apologize to Janae for burping. I told him I would, but I knew deep in my heart that there was no way I was ever going to talk to Janae again. Nope, I had blown my chance, and now I would grow up alone, live alone, and never speak to another girl.

I would become one of those ancient hermits who lives in the mountains and has a bug-filled beard.

ONCE WHEN I WAS A YOUNG BOY, I TALKED TO A GIRL. IT DIDN'T END WELL.

Things got even more uncomfortable for me when I took the bus home and Wonkenstein wouldn't stop wiggling around in my backpack. I guess he was tired of being in there and was trying to stretch. He kept moving and rocking, and so as not to make people suspicious, I had to keep wiggling around myself to make it look like I was the one causing the backpack to shake. One kid thought I was having a fit, and a couple of girls thought I was dancing. Then Wonk began to grunt, so I had to pretend like I was singing to cover it up.

Janae wouldn't even turn her head in my direction. In fact, when we reached our bus stop, she got off so fast she looked like a blur. I asked Trevor if he wanted to come over to my house, but he said he needed to hang out with somebody a little less odd. I tried to explain things to him, but he wouldn't listen. He just kept saying that there was no such thing as Wonkenstein over and over.

When I got inside, Tuffin was standing in the middle of the room, watching TV. There was a clipboard hanging around his neck and a note on the board.

The note was from my mom, and it was a list of all the jobs I needed to do to make up for waking her and my father in the middle of the night.

	ROB'S CHORE LIST
①	PICK OUT DEAD LEAVES STUCK IN ROCKS
②	EMPTY TRASH CANS
③	APOLOGIZE TO MR. PANG
④	PLAY WITH TUFFIN EVERY AFTERNOON
⑤	VACUUM OUT CARS
⑥	UNLOAD THE DISHWASHER
⑦	GET ALONG WITH LIBBY
⑧	CLEAN POOL

I spent the rest of the day picking dead leaves out of the rocks in our front yard. It was my least favorite job. But Wonkenstein sat up in a nearby tree and read me parts of *Frankenstein*. Sometimes the monster part of him would take over and he would

have to grunt pages, but he did a pretty good job.
It was kind of weird to have him reading about part
of himself.

NOTHING CONTRIBUTES SO MUCH GRUNT TO TRANQUILIZE THE MIND AS A GRUNT STEADY PURPOSE GRUNT.

Right before I finished picking all the leaves out of
the rocks, a big gust of wind blew them everywhere.
All in all, it was a pretty rotten day, and for some
reason, I had a feeling tomorrow was going to be
even worse.

CHAPTER 12

~~

NOBODY LISTENS ANYMORE

You know, *Frankenstein* is a pretty good book. In fact, I'll go as far as to say that it's way better than the cartoon. Wonkenstein read some of it to me while I was picking up leaves and then I read some to him before bed. It turns out Trevor was right about Frankenstein being the doctor, not the monster. I kept thinking about Willy Wonka and the candy that had saved us. I thought about the monster that Frankenstein had built and how sad and lonely he was. He kind of reminded me of Ogre.

When I woke up in the morning, both books were still on my mind.

I put Wonkenstein in my backpack again, but this time I gave him a juice box instead of a soda. I thought about leaving Wonk at home, but he said he liked the backpack and that it made him feel like an Oompa-Loompa in its sleeping pod. He also promised that if I took him to school, he would behave. So I crammed Wonk into my pack, heaved him onto my back, and stumbled out of my house. Luckily I didn't fall asleep on the bus again. Today it was Jack's turn to snore and get picked on.

Janae was sitting near the front of the bus, reading a book and pretending people like me didn't exist. I tried to say something to her, but she wouldn't listen. Trevor told me that he had heard from his mom, who had heard from Janae's mother, who had heard from Janae's sister, who had heard from Janae, that I had burped in her face. I told Trevor that it was Wonkenstein, but he didn't believe me.

YOU REALLY SHOULDN'T BLAME THINGS ON HIM. I HEARD IT STRAIGHT FROM MY MOM THAT IT WAS YOU.

I told Trevor about the Awful House and Mr. Pang and Ogre, but he just plugged his ears and said I should stop making things up. I felt pretty bad that even he didn't believe me.

When we got to school, I woke up Jack and asked him why he was so tired. He said his mom had gotten really mad because she couldn't find his little sister's dance costume and some of her good necklaces. He also said they were awake all night searching the house. When I reminded Jack that he had put those things on Wonkenstein, and that I had left them in Ogre's room, he seemed surprised.

The school morning was long, and the clock seemed to be going backward. It got even worse when Principal Smelt pulled me aside in the hall and asked me if I had given up burping.

YES.

GOOD FOR YOU, YOUNG MAN.

The cafeteria served meat loaf and cooked carrots for lunch. The meal left such a greasy feeling in my mouth that I had to drink two sodas to get rid of the taste. Then I really had to burp. I was so scared about getting caught that I went out back during the end of lunch to belch in private. I had just positioned myself to let one rip when I heard Jack's

big brother, Harry, talking to someone behind the
Dumpster by the high school parking lot:

The high school was almost two blocks away, but
their overflow parking lot was right next to our bike
racks. Only the kids who were late ever parked there.
So occasionally groups of long-haired teenagers
would hang out in the parking lot and laugh at us.

Jack's brother stepped out from behind the
Dumpster, and I could see he was talking to Ogre.
Things didn't look right, but there was no way I was

going to say anything to a couple of bigger kids who were talking angrily. Last time a kid from my school had talked to someone in the overflow parking lot, it hadn't ended well.

WOULD YOU PLEASE STOP SALUTING ME AND GO GET HELP?

After lunch period, I walked through the doors to go to my next class and ran into Principal Smelt again. I tried to just pass by, but he stopped to congratulate me on signing up to recite a poem during the assembly. I wanted to tell him that it was all a mistake and that I wasn't going to recite anything, but I was too scared to open my mouth. I hadn't been able to burp because of Jack's brother and Ogre being there, and I was worried that if I even cracked my lips, something unknown would slip out.

Just so you know, I'm not one of those kids who likes to belch in public—I definitely don't want that reputation. There are enough things I feel awkward about already. I just stood there with my mouth closed as Principal Smelt told me about all the character I was going to gain by reading a dramatic poem. I got away before he sang a song about it.

I couldn't figure out what was wrong with me. I felt bad about a lot of the things going on, and the problem kept coming back to Wonkenstein. I knew there was no way I could keep bringing him to school in my backpack and pretending everything was fine. I had never talked to Principal Smelt before, and now I had talked to him three times in the last two days. Trevor was staying away from me. Janae couldn't even look at me. My parents were disappointed in me and filling my free time with chores. Plus, I was expected to recite a dramatic poem in front of my entire school in a couple of weeks.

In my last class of the day, Wonkenstein kept whispering things to me from inside of the backpack.

I tried to whisper to him to be quiet, but after the tenth time, my teacher stopped me.

I wanted to tell them that they should all look away, but I was too embarrassed. Besides, I was still trying not to belch. My stomach was turning and gurgling as I sat there. I could feel my face getting warm, and Wonkenstein was shifting uncomfortably in my backpack and digging one of his small elbows into my spine. I was actually about to pass out when Scott Millford saved me. Scott was sitting three rows away, and apparently the greasy lunch wasn't sitting well with him either. But while it was making me want to burp, it made him fart.

Poor Scott just sat there with his face bright red while everyone scooted away. I felt bad, but I was happy for the distraction. My teacher never came back to me, and the bell rang five minutes later. I made sure to thank Scott on the way out, but I don't think he thought I was being serious.

On the bus ride home, Janae still ignored me, and Trevor sat by Jack. I had to sit down by Overfriendly Todd. Todd was always friendly, but he had just eaten two cupcakes, so he was really amped up.

I ignored Todd while Wonkenstein whispered to me the ingredients for making a candy that would temporarily change the color of a person's eyes. He then grunted twice and started to whimper while whispering the name Justine. I knew from reading *Frankenstein* that he was just worried about a girl he liked. It kind of made me feel a little better to know that we were both having girl trouble. It didn't fix everything, but it helped.

CHAPTER 13

FROM BAD TO WORSE

The last few weeks have been weird, painful, and weird again. Every day, I've stuffed Wonk in my backpack and taken him to school. He's learned to stay perfectly quiet and my back's gotten stronger, but aside from that, things are at an all-time low.

I've needed Trevor's help to figure out what to do with Wonkenstein and to understand why he's even here, but Trevor's not up for it. Janae still won't talk to me. I guess the burp and the fake dancing on the

bus were enough for her to write me off completely.
My biggest problem is trying to keep Wonk hidden.
It's not easy to find new places to hide him.

While I like being with Wonk, I can't figure out
what I'm going to do with him for the rest of my
life. I've thought about starting a circus and having
him be the star, but the only other acts I could
think of were lame.

I kind of want to tell my parents about Wonk, but they're still pretty mad at me. I thought it would wear off after the first week, but they are sticking to their disappointment. Twice I've broken down and almost told them, but both times they interrupted me and gave me more chores.

I tried to apologize to Mr. Pang, but every time I started walking over to his house, I would chicken out and go a different direction. I always ended up somewhere completely unrelated.

Wonk and I spent a lot of time alone, hanging out in my room and reading. We finally finished *Frankenstein*. The green part of Wonk really got into it. I thought it was long and full of hard words, but I still liked it. The only bad part was that I now felt like the monster in the book—nobody understood or wanted to be around me.

To make matters worse, today over the intercom Principal Smelt announced that the dramatic poetry contest is tomorrow. He even read off the names of the seven participants. To my horror, I was still one of them. I had been too embarrassed to talk to Janae and tell her to cross my name off the list.

~~ROBERT BURNSIDE~~

Also, when I got off the bus, I couldn't help but notice the cop car in front of the Awful House. Its motor was running, and its lights were flashing. There were two cops out front, talking to Mr. Pang

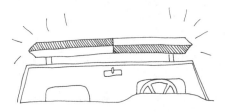

and Ogre. I needed to find out what was going on. I ran into my house, tossed my backpack on my bed, and unzipped it. Wonkenstein crawled out and began to stretch. I told him to stay put and opened my window. I would have climbed out, but my mom hollered at me through my bedroom door. It kind of sounded like my door was haunted and speaking to me. Of course, I don't think any truly haunted door would ever say anything like . . .

I was spooked, but it was only because I hated unloading the dishwasher. I raced to the kitchen and put the dishes away in record time. I was going so fast, I accidentally smacked Libby on the head with a plastic bowl.

She yelled at me as I slammed the dishwasher closed and ran out to the rock island. The cop car was still there, and my friends were hunched down behind the bushes, watching.

Teddy started talking faster than I could listen. He said something about Jack's brother, Harry, catching Ogre with some stolen necklace. And Jack's mother had called the police, and Mr. Pang had gotten into a fight with the cops. Now Ogre was going to a prison where he would have to break up rocks with a pickax for the rest of his life.

The cops got into their car and pulled away. Rourk was cheering, and Aaron was making siren noises, but I was worried. Ogre didn't steal any necklace. It was kind of Wonkenstein's fault, and for some reason Wonkenstein was my fault. I had to make things right. The problem was that I was too chicken to do anything.

BAAAKAAK!!

I slowly shuffled back to my house. Libby was still in the kitchen, whining about how I had ruined her beautiful hairstyle. I couldn't take it anymore and I went to my room. Wonkenstein sat on my pillow and sang me a song while patting me on the head. It didn't make me feel any better.

MR. ROB IS NICE, MR. ROB IS GOOD...

I wanted to fall asleep and wake up feeling less guilty. I thought about all my problems. I thought about the poetry competition and began to think up ways I could get out of going to school tomorrow. I couldn't come up with a good disease to use.

I tested my closet door again, but it was still locked, and Beardy had his eyes closed.

Tuffin came into my room, smiling.

I picked Wonkenstein up off my bed and put him on the floor. I then gave them one of my blankets.

They both seemed excited to get a blanket to play with. I lay back down on my bed. I was going to close my eyes and think of other sicknesses I could fake when a thought hit me. It was a scary thought, so I shoved it away in my mind. But it kept popping back up.

I argued with myself for a while before I finally gave in to my brain. I wasn't happy about it, but I knew what I had to do. If nobody would listen to me, it was the only way. I reluctantly walked out of my room, and before my mom could tell me to do more jobs, I invited her to come hear my poem tomorrow.

My mom was so shocked she had to close her book and take a breather. I went to my room and kicked Tuffin out. I got *Charlie and the Chocolate Factory*, sat on the floor, and flipped through it with Wonk. I showed him kind of what I wanted to write, and he smiled.

CHAPTER 14

DRAMA

A couple of years ago, I had a speaking part in my school's Thanksgiving play. I was supposed to walk out onstage dressed as a corncob and say . . .

I'M ALL EARS.

Then the crowd would laugh, and I was supposed to walk over and join the rest of the fruits and vegetables in the huge cornucopia. But I was nervous, and when I walked out onto the stage, I froze. I just stood there until a large gourd came over and ushered me off. Right before I reached the edge of the stage, I screamed out . . .

Ever since then, I've been more than just a little bit scared to speak in public. The very idea makes my heart race wildly.

Now not only was I going to have to speak in public, but unless I did a good job, I was going to end up in more trouble than I was in already. Wonkenstein kept telling me that I would do well. To be honest, though, I don't think he really understood what was at stake. We had stayed up late working, but I knew that didn't guarantee success.

Right after my first class, I ran into Teddy. He knew today was the day I was going to recite a poem at the assembly, and he wanted to make fun of me before anyone else did.

Teddy was the first to make fun of me, but he wasn't the last. People I didn't even know started to tease me. It wasn't too late to get out of it. I knew I could just go to the nurse and tell her I had lost my voice or that I could no longer walk. But I also knew that this was my *best* chance to make a few things right.

Nelson Spillbrick cornered me near the broken drinking fountain and demanded to know what I was doing. He was one of the other participants in the poetry contest, and apparently he took this stuff seriously.

YOU'RE NOT GOING TO RUIN THIS FOR ME. THIS IS MY MOMENT.

IS THAT CAPE PART OF YOUR MOMENT?

FOR YOUR INFORMATION, I ALWAYS WEAR A CAPE DURING MY PERFORMANCES.

I was going to point out that most normal people don't wear capes, but I thought about my Thumb Buddies and figured I should just keep my mouth shut.

The assembly was during the last hour of the school day. I was growing more and more sure that my plan had no chance of working. When I got to the auditorium, Janae, Nelson, and the four other participants were practicing backstage.

I was about to say something witty to Janae when Mr. Cartel, the drama teacher, came up to me singing . . .

YOU MUST BE ROBERTO!

ACT OUT

Mr. Cartel told me I couldn't wear my backpack while performing. I told him I needed it and that it was kind of like my security blanket. Janae looked embarrassed to even know me. Mr. Cartel said there was no security in dramatic poetry readings. I panicked for a second, knowing I needed to have Wonkenstein nearby. Luckily, I thought of a solution:

Mr. Cartel took off his odd hat and put seven small pieces of paper in it. We then drew numbers to see what order we would perform in. I got number . . . 7 .

I could hear hundreds of kids coming into the auditorium, and when I looked out of the curtains, I almost threw up. The worst part was that Teddy, Aaron, Trevor, Rourk, and Jack were all sitting in the front row. I could also see my parents seated with Tuffin. This was a terrible idea.

I walked to the far back corner and took off my backpack. I set it on the floor and unzipped the top just a bit.

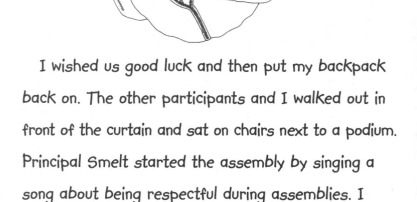

THIS IS EXCITING! YOUR FACE LOOKS AS GREEN AS PART OF MINE

I wished us good luck and then put my backpack back on. The other participants and I walked out in front of the curtain and sat on chairs next to a podium. Principal Smelt started the assembly by singing a song about being respectful during assemblies. I don't think most people were paying attention.

WOOOOO!

ROCK CRUSHES SCISSORS.

HEY MARY!

There were three judges sitting at a table. Either they were all Oompa-Loompas or the table was too tall, because I could barely see their heads.

Nelson went first and dramatically recited a poem about a kid who loved horses better than people.

I couldn't believe this was Nelson's moment. I guess the judges were liking it because I think they gave him a pretty good score. I couldn't tell for sure, though, because they all seemed to be using a different grade scale.

The next guy only said eleven words, but he said them so slowly and with such long pauses between each word that it felt longer. He also kept hugging himself.

THE — WORLD — IS —
— IN — NEED —
- OF — LOVE, — SO
HUG — HUG — HUG.

He then bowed about twenty times. His score was a little vaguer than the last.

The first girl acted out a dramatic poem about a kid who wanted to be president but settled for being a dentist. I couldn't understand where they were getting these awful poems to recite. The next girl performed a poem about a seed that grew up to be a tree that got chopped down and made into a table. A boy named Peter Hill acted out a made-up *Star Wars* scene with a weird happy ending. He was wearing a robe, and for some reason, he stood on a chair. The *Star Wars* scene was embarrassing, but at least he was talking about a movie I knew.

His score was a little better than the first four contestants'.

Janae was fantastic, of course. She recited a poem about a horse that was sick. By the end of it,

I felt for the poor horse. I think her score was the best so far.

When she sat back down, I just stared at her. Eventually Principal Smelt fake coughed and brought me out of my trance. I glanced around, and the whole audience was looking at me. My mom had her hand over her eyes, and Rourk was making a face. This was crazy. My idea seemed good last night, but now I thought drawing inspiration from a book might have been a bad idea.

The three judges were already scribbling things down. I stood up slowly and walked to the podium. I sniffed twice and announced the name of my poem.

I'd thought people would clap, but it was so quiet I could actually hear the crickets that were in an empty aquarium in the science room.

I looked out at the crowd again and tried to count all the people who would beat me up later for doing this. I thought about just standing there until someone

pushed me off the stage, but Wonkenstein pinched
me through the backpack and
jolted me out of my silence. I
cleared my throat, and the
microphone screeched.

AHHHHH!!

I waited until everyone stopped
screaming and then started my poem again.

Misunderstandings.
Dear friends, we surely all must say
misunderstandings block the way
of others knowing what you mean
or parents seeing what you've seen...

Like so many times in my life, my mind froze.

FROZEN MIND*

NOW WITH 50% MORE PEAS

* THAN BEFORE USING

I had written the poem in the style of the Oompa-Loompa songs, but now I couldn't remember the words. I stared at the audience, wishing they would have the courtesy to just get up and leave. Right then I could hear something over my right shoulder. It was Wonk whispering my next line from the backpack.

... about a thing the other day.
I might have made my parents sad,
and woke my sleeping mom and dad,
but if they knew the day I had,
they probably wouldn't be so mad.

I looked at my mom and dad, and to my surprise, they were both smiling.

I looked at Janae, gulped, and continued.

Or say somebody thought you belched,
but it wasn't you; t'was someone else.
How do you tell a next-door friend
it wasn't you who broke mouth wind?

Janae was laughing. I couldn't believe it. In fact, most of the audience was beginning to laugh as well.

And what if someone who lives nearby—
a sort of big and scary guy—

is blamed for stealing something from
a different neighbor whose son's a bum.

I looked at Jack and tried to give
him the very best stink eye I could.

Well, maybe I could help that bum
and fix the thing that he made wrong.
We could clear that Ogre's name
and properly place the misplaced blame.
Misunderstandings between friends
are out of style and never in,
like bell-bottoms and mustaches,

Thumb Buddies and real thick glasses.

So to those of you I might have hurt
I hope you know I feel like dirt.
But try and understand that I
am really not an awful guy.

And now, in closing, let me say
the main misunderstanding that's come my way:
I once thought books were kinda boring;
I thought they caused both sleep and snoring.

It took a monster and a tinker
to show me I was such a stinker,
to make me get up off my rear
and do some things I usually fear.

All those pages of words and letters

actually made my life much better.

So next time you think you understand

or that you've got the upper hand,

remember, things are better off

if misunderstandings are all cleared up.

Wonkenstein reached out his hands and pulled on two party poppers to signal the end of my poem. Confetti and tiny streamers flew up, and the crowd went wild.

SOFTROCK
MIDDLE
SCHOOL
POETRY
CONTEST

I couldn't believe how good I felt. The monster part of Wonkenstein thrashed about in the backpack due to the noise, while the Wonka part cheered along with everyone else.

The judges held up their scores.

I **WON!** Nelson stormed up and accused me of stealing his moment, but everyone else patted me on the shoulder. The prize was a golden lunch ticket that gave me free school lunches for the rest of the year.

It was nice, but I didn't do it for the ticket.

I did it for Janae.

CHAPTER 15

THE CLOSET

Most of my friends congratulated me. Only Teddy gave me a hard time.

I LIKED YOU BETTER AS CORN.

Jack promised to go with me to apologize to Mr. Pang. At first he said no, but when I told him that it would make us feel better and that he could bring his assault flashlight, he agreed.

My mom hugged me and called me Ribert in front of everyone, but I was too pumped up to be embarrassed. We then went out for celebration ice cream. It was pretty good, but I really just wanted to get home so I could let Wonk out of my backpack. My dad kept saying how proud he was. He also kept winking and making jokes about misunderstandings. When I told him I should probably go home and do homework, he said . . .

WELL, THEN, LET'S GET YOU HOME. WE WOULDN'T WANT TO MISUNDERSTAND YOU.

When I got home, I went straight to my room and freed Wonk. He tumbled out of the backpack with a huge grunt. I couldn't *believe* how relieved I was. I *stood up*, and Wonkenstein wrapped his arms around my right leg. I was just about to ask him if he wanted to go with me to Trevor's house to pay him the five dollars I owed him when I heard . . .

My heart dropped, and I could feel it fall all the way into my *big toe.*

I looked over at the closet as the heavy door creaked and opened about an inch. I glanced down at Wonkenstein as he gazed up at me.

LOOKS LIKE MY TIME IS UP. I'M OFF TO THE NORTH POLE. OR MAYBE I'LL VISIT THE FACTORY.

Wonkenstein let go of my leg and walked over to the closet. He pulled the closet door open.

In a flash, he slipped in and the door closed behind him with a click. It all happened so fast my brain didn't really have time to process what was going on.

FAREWELL -GRUNT- ROBERT. -GRUNT- LATER, FRIEND.

I stepped over to the closet and took hold of
Beardy. The knob turned, and I pulled the door open,
expecting to see Wonkenstein. But all I saw was
junk—nothing but junk.

I looked around, wondering if my eyes were playing tricks on me, but it was clear they weren't— Wonkenstein was gone. I could see a large jar of goo from my old lab dripping down over a tall pile of books. There on the top of the books was a copy of *Frankenstein*, sitting on a copy of *Charlie and the Chocolate Factory*. I looked at the books and the goo and all the rest of the mess in the closet, but there was no sign of Wonk.

I closed the closet door and checked under the bed and in my dresser.

ALL RIGHT, YOU CAN STOP MESSING AROUND. WHERE ARE YOU?

When I tried to open the closet door again, it wouldn't budge. I pulled and pulled, but just like before, it wouldn't open. I pounded and hollered and kicked, but it was stuck tight. I was yelling about the North Pole when my father came into the room to see what was going on. I told him everything was fine.

JUST ANOTHER MISUNDERSTANDING, HUH?

My dad left and Tuffin came into my room to tell me it was time for us to play. I spun him around until he was dizzy. For added fun, I instructed him to count until tomorrow.

I then lay down on my bed to read.

CHAPTER 16

KNOCK KNOCK

Life just wasn't the same without Wonk. I mean, I had wanted him to get back into the closet, but now I missed him. I hadn't even *been* able to say good-bye. I knew from what he had said *before* he went into the closet that he was going to the worlds of the books he had come from.

The day after Wonk disappeared, Trevor and I tried to get the closet open with a bunch of stuff like a crowbar and a shovel, but it didn't work. We just ended up breaking everything.

Jack and I apologized to Mr. Pang and tried to explain what had happened. He didn't buy it. Instead, he made us weed his dead flower garden. He also promised that if we ever trespassed again, he would sic Ogre on us. We said okay, but I now knew Ogre really wasn't somebody to fear.

Every time I went into my room, I wiggled the closet doorknob, hoping it would open and Wonk would be there. It was never open, which meant Wonkenstein was never there. It made me pretty sad. I figured my closet would just stay shut forever. But four nights later, as I was reading, I heard a knock I didn't recognize.

THUMP

I thought it was somebody at my bedroom door, so I hollered for them to "come in." Nobody did. I went back to reading, and I heard a louder, blocky knock.

THUMP

I got up from my bed and marched to my door. I threw it open, but nobody was there. I walked down the hall and saw that Tuffin was asleep in his room. Libby's door was shut, and I could hear her talking on the phone. My parents had gone to a movie, so I knew it couldn't have been them, and Puck was out in the backyard.

I was thinking about how I probably should just go to sleep early and give my mind a rest when I heard a sharp, biting knock coming from my closet.

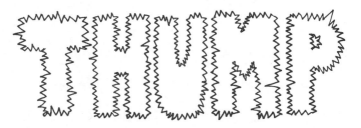

I spun around and looked at my closet door as my heart beat like crazy.

I moved closer to my closet, reached out, and grabbed Beardy. I turned the knob and heard it click as it opened. The heavy door moved forward,

and something sprang out and knocked me over.
My head hit the end of my bed as I fell to the
floor. Whatever it was was now moving around on
top of my dresser. I turned over quickly, expecting
to see Wonk. It wasn't Wonk, and it wasn't normal!
The creature was a little smaller than Wonkenstein
but a lot hairier. He looked like a Chewbacca and
Harry Potter hybrid. He whispered something about
wizards and wars while waving a wand and growling.
He then called me by name and informed me that
Wonk had sent him. I just stood there and wobbled
as he asked . . .

SO, WHERE SHOULD WE BEGIN?

The only answer I could think of was "the library."

COMING SOON

POTTERWOOKIEE

THE CREATURE
FROM MY
CLOSET

Book II

OBERT SKYE is the author of the two bestselling fantasy adventure series Leven Thumps and The Pillage Trilogy. As a kid, he spent many hours in detention for drawing on his school desks (not advised). It wasn't all bad—in fifth grade he won ten dollars and tickets to the circus for his drawing of a clown (actually drawn on paper). Today, there are few scraps of paper or surfaces in his life that don't have ink on them. *Wonkenstein* brings together Obert's love of comics and storytelling. He hopes this book will earn him some brownie points (or forgiveness) with his past teachers whose desks he marked up. He lives in Idaho with his family.

abituneven.com